Australia 2c

tales from
outer
suburbia

tales from outer suburbia

shaun tan

templar publishing

templar publishing

VIA AIR MA
PAR AVIO

70700 KUOPIO
11.11.-1999

TO PAUL,
(who always enjoys
a good expedition)
PERTH, W.A.

PRIORITY
[1. luokka - 1 klass]

CONTENTS

the water buffalo

when I was a kid, there was a big water buffalo living in the vacant lot at the end of our street, the one with the grass no one ever mowed. He slept most of the time, and ignored everybody who walked past, unless we happened to stop and ask him for advice. Then he would come up to us slowly, raise his left hoof and literally point us in the right direction. But he never said what he was pointing at, or how far we had to go, or what we were supposed to do once we got there. In fact, he never said anything because water buffalos are like that; they hate talking.

This was too frustrating for most of us. By the time anyone thought to 'consult the buffalo', our problem was usually urgent and required a straightforward and immediate solution. Eventually we stopped visiting him altogether, and I think he went away some time after that: all we could see was long grass.

It's a shame, really, because whenever we had followed his pointy hoof we'd always been surprised, relieved and delighted at what we found. And every time we'd said exactly the same thing – 'How did he know?'

eric

some years ago we had a foreign exchange student come
to live with us. We found it very difficult to pronounce
his name correctly, but he didn't mind.
He told us to just call him 'Eric'.

We had repainted the spare room, bought new rugs and furniture
and generally made sure everything would be comfortable
for him. So I can't say why it was that Eric chose to sleep and
study most of the time in our kitchen pantry.

'It must be a cultural thing,' said Mum. 'As long as he is happy.'
We started storing food and kitchen things in other
cupboards so we wouldn't disturb him.

But sometimes I wondered if Eric *was* happy; he was so polite
that I'm not sure he would have told us if something bothered him.
A few times I saw him through the pantry door gap, studying with silent
intensity, and imagined what it might be like for him here in our country.

Secretly I had been looking forward to having a foreign visitor
– I had so many things to show him. For once I could be a local
expert, a fountain of interesting facts and opinions. Fortunately,
Eric was very curious and always had plenty of questions.

However, they weren't the kind of questions I had been expecting.

Most of the time I could only say,
'I'm not really sure,' or, 'That's just how it is.'
I didn't feel very helpful at all.

I had planned for us to go on a number of weekly
excursions together, as I was determined to show our
visitor the best places in the city and its surrounds.
I think Eric enjoyed these trips, but once again,
it was hard to really know.

Most of the time Eric seemed more interested in small things he discovered on the ground.

I might have found this a little exasperating, but I kept thinking about what Mum had said, about the cultural thing.
Then I didn't mind so much.

Nevertheless, none of us could help but be bewildered by the way Eric left our home: a sudden departure early one morning, with little more than a wave and a polite goodbye.

It actually took us a while to realise he wasn't coming back.

There was much speculation over dinner later that evening. Did Eric seem upset? Did he enjoy his stay? Would we ever hear from him again?

An uncomfortable feeling hung in the air, like something unfinished, unresolved. It bothered us for hours, or at least until one of us discovered what was in the pantry.

Go and see for yourself: it's still there after all these years, thriving in the darkness. It's the first thing we show any new visitors to our house. 'Look what our foreign exchange student left for us,' we tell them.

'It must be a cultural thing,' says Mum.

broken
toys

i know you think you saw him first, but I'm pretty sure it was me – he was over there by the underpass, feeling his way along the graffiti-covered wall and, I said, 'Look, there's something you don't see every day.'

Well, we'd certainly seen crazy people before – 'shell-shocked by life' as you once put it. But something pretty strange must have happened to this guy to make him decide to wander about in a spacesuit on a dead-quiet public holiday. We hid behind a postbox to get a better look. Up close it was even more perplexing, the spacesuit was covered in barnacles and sea-stuff, and dripping wet in spite of the fierce summer heat.

'It's not a spacesuit, stupid,' you whispered. 'It's that old-fashioned diving gear, from the pearlers up north. You know, in the olden days, when they got the *bends* because they didn't know about decompressification and how it turns your blood into lemonade.' You sighed loudly at my blank look and said, 'Never mind.'

But, as we stealthily followed our crazy person, I could tell you were right, because of the helmet, and the long air hose dragging behind.

He shuffled aimlessly across the empty football oval, past the petrol station and up and down people's driveways. He plodded around the edge of the closed corner deli, feeling along walls and windows as if sleepwalking, leaving big wet glove-prints that dried to ghostly patches of salt.

You said, 'I'll give you *ten bucks* to go and say hello.'

I said, 'No way.'

'We'll both go then.'

'Okay.'

We crept closer. The smell was weird, like the ocean, I suppose, but with some other sweet odour that was hard to identify. Red dust had collected in the creases of the suit, as though he had been through a desert as well as an ocean.

We were strategically planning our opening remarks when the dull, scratched face-plate turned towards us and said something we couldn't make out. The diver moved forwards, creaking, babbling. We backed off.

'Crazy talk,' I said.

But you listened carefully and shook your head. 'Nah, I think it's... *Japanese.*'

He was saying the same sentence over and over – ending with something like 'tasoo-ke-te, tasoo-ke-te.' And he was holding out one hand to show us a little wooden horse, which might once have been golden and shiny, but was now cracked and sun-bleached, held together with string.

'Maybe we should take him to Mrs Bad News,' you suggested, meaning old Mrs Katayama, the only Japanese person we knew in our neighbourhood.

'No way,' I said, and my raised eyebrows referred to our all-too-recent confrontation over the back fence, best described as a barrage of incomprehensible abuse followed by the return of our model aeroplane sliced neatly in half – a further addition to our box of stray toys that had fallen into the old crone's backyard and come back dissected. These were the only times we ever saw her, hence, 'Mrs Bad News'.

Your raised eyebrows referred to exactly the same thing, but also signalled the flash of a brilliant idea. Why not lead a crazy man in a diving suit to Mrs Katayama's front yard, and lock him in? Nothing more needed to be said. We did the Special Handshake of Unbreakable Agreement.

You reached out to take the diver's enormous gloved hand, then suddenly recoiled – 'It was so weird and slimy,' you explained later – yet our guy understood enough to follow, shuffling along footpaths, across roads and down back-alley short-cuts. His long, wheezy breathing grew louder each time we stopped to let him catch up. He plodded behind us as if every joint ached, with that big hose dragging behind, trickling a seemingly endless supply of water from its frayed end. It gave me the creeps.

Finally we arrived at the dreaded house with the overgrown cherry trees. We ushered our guest through the front gate, which we had long ago figured out how to unlock. The weathered steps creaked under his weight. You rattled the flyscreen door, and then we both got the hell out of there. We snapped the gate shut behind us, barely able to suppress our giggles, and ran behind the phone booth on the other side of the road to behold the unfolding drama.

We waited and waited.

And waited.

'This sucks,' you eventually admitted, remembering that Mrs Bad News never opened her door, even though she was always home. We had often joked that the door was painted onto the front wall. We had tried knocking once before, and she had just yelled, 'Who Is There?' and then 'Go Away!' Such was the experience of our diver friend on this occasion. But he did not move, perhaps because he did not understand, so there was still hope for entertainment.

Suddenly the diver reached up, removed his heavy helmet and let it slip from his hands to the wooden boards with a loud bang that made us jump. Even from behind we could see he was a young man with neatly combed hair, shiny black. A far more surprising sight was the front door opening, and the frail silhouette of Mrs Bad News peeking through.

The diver said those Japanese words again and held out the toy horse. He was blocking our view so we couldn't see much, except Mrs Bad News covering her mouth with both hands. She looked like she was about to faint from terror. We couldn't believe our luck.

'Hang on a sec,' you said, squinting, 'I think she's…*crying!*' And indeed she was – standing in her doorway, sobbing uncontrollably.

Had we gone too far?

We actually started feeling *bad* for her… But then her pale matchstick arms flew out and wrapped around the wet, barnacled figure on her doorstep. We didn't see what happened next because we were too busy comparing our raised eyebrows of disbelief. Then the flyscreen door slapped shut and there was only the dark rectangle of the doorway, with the diving helmet sitting in a puddle of water.

We waited a long time, but nothing else happened.

'I guess she knew him,' I said as we walked home around the corner.

We never found out who the diver was, or what happened to him. But we had started hearing old-style jazz wafting over the back fence late in the evenings, and we noticed funny cooking smells and soft-spoken voices in animated conversation. And we stopped hating Mrs Katayama after that, because she would come all the way around to our front door with a quiet nod and a quick smile, returning our stray toys just as we had lost them – all in one piece.

14

HAVE YOU EVER WONDERED
WHAT HAPPENS TO ALL THE
POEMS PEOPLE WRITE?

the poems they never
let anyone else read?   ...

PERHAPS THEY ARE
TOO PRIVATE AND PERSONAL.

Perhaps they are just not good enoug

Perhaps the prospect
of such a heartfelt
expression being seen as

CLUMSY

Shallow   silly

PRETENTIOUS   Saccharine

UNORIGINAL   sentimental

trite

boring

Overwrought   OBSCURE   STUPID

pointless

OR

simply embarrassing

is enough to give any aspiring
Poet good reason to
hide their work from
public view.

forever.

sday, January 1, 1964.   (Registered at the G.P.O.
transmission by post as a

mu s   čka vře-14

Naturally many poems are IMMEDIATELY DESTROYED

BURNT

shredded

flushed away

OCCASIONALLY THEY ARE FOLDED
INTO LITTLE SQUARES
AND WEDGED UNDER THE CORNER OF
AN UNSTABLE PIECE OF FURNITURE

(so actually quite useful)

2

OTHERS ARE
HIDDEN BEHIND
A LOOSE BRICK

or drainpipe   or

OR

put between the pages of
AN OBSCURE BOOK
that is unlikely
to ever be opened.

Sealed into
the back of an
old alarm clock

someone might
find them
one day,   BUT PROBABLY NOT

The truth is that unread poetry
will almost always be *just that*

well

doomed   to join the a vast, invisible river
of waste that flows out of suburbia.

Almost always.

On rare occasions,

Some especially insistent pieces of writing will escape

INTO A BACKYARD OR A LANEWAY

be blown along a roadside embankment

and finally come to rest in a shopping centre car park

as so many things do

It is here that something quite F Remarkable takes place

two or more pieces of poetry drift towards each other

through a strange force of attraction

UNKNOWN TO SCIENCE

and ever so slowly cling together to form a tiny, shapeless ball.

LEFT UNDISTURBED, THIS BALL GRADUALLY BECOMES LARGER AND ROUNDER AS OTHER free verses

confessions ~~secre~~ Secrets

stray musings Wishes and unsent love letters

attach themselves one by one

Such a ball creeps
through the streets
LIKE A TUMBLEWEED
for months   even years

IF IT COMES OUT ONLY AT NIGHT IT HAS A GOOD
CHANCE OF SURVIVING TRAFFIC AND CHILDREN

and through a
slow rolling motion   AVOIDS SNAILS
(its number one predator)

At a certain size, it instinctively
shelters from bad weather, unnoticed

but otherwise roams the streets,

searching
for scraps
of forgotten
thought and feeling.

GIVEN
TIME + LUCK   the poetry ball becomes

large HUGE ENORMOUS:

A VAST ACCUMULATION OF PAPERY BITS
THAT ULTIMATELY TAKES TO THE AIR, LEVITATING BY
THE SHEER FORCE OF SO MUCH UNSPOKEN EMOTION.

It floats gently
above suburban rooftops
when everybody is asleep   inspiring lonely dogs
to bark in the middle
of the night.

Sadly

a big ball of paper,
no matter how large and
buoyant, is still a *fragile thing*

SOONER OR
LATER

it will be surprised by

a sudden
gust of wind

BEATEN BY

driving   rain

and

REDUCED

in a matter
of minutes

to

a billion

soggy

SHREDS

One morning

everyone will wake up
to find a pulpy mess
covering front lawns

CLOGGING UP GUTTERS

and plastering car
windscreens

Traffic will be delayed

Children Delighted

adults BAFFLED

unable to figure out   where it all came from

STRANGER STILL
WILL BE THE
DISCOVERY THAT
EVERY LUMP OF
WET PAPER
CONTAINS VARIOUS faded words pressed into accidental
verse

BARELY VISIBLE,
BUT UNDENIABLY
PRESENT

To each reader
they will whisper
something different

SOMETHING

joyful   Something sad

TRUTHFUL   absurd

hilarious

PROFOUND   and perfect.

No one will be able to explain the

strange feeling of weightlessness

or the private smile
that remains

Long after the street sweepers
have come and gone.

undertow

the house at number seventeen was only ever mentioned with lowered voices by the neighbours. They knew well the frequent sounds of shouting, slamming doors and crashing objects. But one sultry summer night, something else happened, something far more interesting: the appearance of a large marine animal on the front lawn.

By midmorning, all the neighbours had spotted this mysterious, gently breathing creature. Naturally, they gathered around for a better look.

'It's a dugong,' said a small boy. 'The dugong is a rare and endangered plant-eating mammal that lives in the Indian Ocean, of the order Sirenia, family Dugongidae, genus *dugong*, species *D. dugong*.'

None of which explained how it came to be in their street, at least four kilometres from the nearest beach. In any case, the neighbours were far more concerned with attending to the stranded animal using buckets, hoses and wet blankets, just as they had seen whale-rescuers do on TV.

When the young couple who lived at number seventeen finally emerged to survey the scene, bleary-eyed and confused, their immediate impulse was towards anger and recrimination. 'Is this your idea of a JOKE?' they shouted at each other, and at some of the neighbours as well. But this soon gave way to silent bewilderment when challenged by the sheer absurdity of the situation. There was nothing for them to do, but assist the rescue effort by turning on the front sprinklers and calling an appropriate emergency service, if such a thing existed (a matter they debated at some length, impatiently grabbing the phone from each other's hands).

While waiting for the experts, the neighbours took turns to pat and reassure the dugong, speaking to its slowly blinking eye – which struck each of them as being filled with deep sadness – and putting an ear against its warm wet hide to hear something very low and far away, but otherwise indescribable.

The arrival of the rescue truck was an almost unwelcome interruption, with flashing orange lights and council workers in bright yellow overalls ordering everyone to stand back. Their efficiency was impressive: they even had a special kind of hoist and a bath just big enough to comfortably hold a good-sized sea-going mammal. In a matter of minutes they had loaded the dugong into the vehicle and driven away, as if they dealt with this sort of problem all the time.

Later that evening the neighbours switched impatiently between news channels to see if there was any mention of the dugong and, when there wasn't, concluded that the whole event was possibly not as remarkable as they had originally thought.

The couple at number seventeen went back to shouting at each other, this time about fixing the front lawn. The grass that had been underneath the dugong was now unaccountably yellow and dead, as if the creature had been there for years rather than hours. Then the discussion became about something else entirely and an object, maybe a plate, crashed against a wall.

Nobody saw the small boy clutching an encyclopedia of marine zoology leave the front door of that house, creep toward the dugong-shaped patch and lie down in the middle of it, arms by his sides, looking at the clouds and stars, hoping it would be a long time before his parents noticed that he wasn't in his room and came out angry and yelling. How odd it was, then, when they both eventually appeared without a sound, without suddenness. How strange that all he felt were gentle hands lifting him up and carrying him back to bed.

grandpa's story

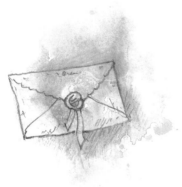

'you know that big hill you can see from your bedroom window?' says Grandpa, pointing. 'Well, your grandma and I got married on the other side of it, long before you lot came along. Of course, weddings were more complicated in those days, not the short 'n' sweet kind you see today.

'For a start, the bride and groom were sent away before the ceremony, and they were only allowed to have one photo taken upon leaving, and no more until they came back, which might be a long time later. That's why there are so many blank pages in our wedding album, "the dark pages" we call them. Lucky for us that first picture came out good. Look at the family, all dressed up on the driveway. Look at your grandma there, as though she's just stepped out of a movie. Talk about stylish.

'After the photographer left, we were given a sealed envelope, a compass and traditional wedding boots – hardy things they were, with steel caps. Each guest told us a special riddle, like a cryptic crossword clue. We had to listen hard and remember them all, strange instructions that would supposedly make sense later on. We were mad keen to get started and figure it all out, so we didn't hang around. We were off!'

Grandpa is a bit vague at this stage in his story, so it's not clear where they actually went. Somewhere 'past the factories and landfills' and 'beyond all the signs and roads'. When we ask him to show us on a map, he simply shakes his head in an amused way, as if to say 'one day you'll know.'

He waves aside our further questions and continues: 'We weren't allowed to open the envelope until we arrived. Inside was a list of objects we had to find before the end of the day, each corresponding to a clue. This was the Scavenger Hunt, always the most troublesome and feared part of any wedding. Well, we expected to be back home and dressed for the well-rehearsed vows in no time at all – we were young and full of confidence, always in a hurry too. Of course, it was not too long before we ran into trouble, a whole lot of trouble…'

Frustratingly, Grandpa goes off to make a cup of tea at this point. We follow him to the kitchen and press for details. Grandpa just shrugs. 'It's hard to explain the terrible things that happened out there. In fact, the more I tell you, the less you will actually understand. Some things in life are like that. You have to find out for yourself…

'They were perilous times. But every setback only made us more determined. Scared? Sure, sometimes, but we had each other. That must be what it's all about, we thought: as long as we stick together, nothing can stop us!

'And true enough, one by one we found those objects on the list. It was hard work and we had trouble remembering some of the clues. But there was a lot of happiness discovering so many small things in unexpected places. We tied everything to the rear bumper with wedding string in the customary way.

'The sound of that rattling from the back of the car was very satisfying at first, but really started to get on our nerves after hours and hours of driving around. It was late by then, and we had a big problem. A really big problem. You see, the last two objects on our list seemed impossible to find, and I think both of us were beginning to wonder if they even existed. Yet we couldn't return unless we found them. We searched and searched, wracked our brains and did everything we were supposed to. Still nothing.

'We became anxious, desperate, obsessed, driving further and faster, not thinking about where we were going. Eventually we found ourselves lost in a vast magnetic desert, unable to get a reliable compass bearing. My own old grandpa once spoke of "a place all lovers are doomed to visit at least once" – maybe this was what he was talking about, I thought. It was terrible!

'The sun was creeping below the horizon. We would never make it back in time for the vows. We'd missed our big moment. Our smiles vanished. We stopped holding hands. And then – BANG! – the back tyre burst on a pointy rock! Well that was it! Your grandma leapt out, slammed the door furiously and started blaming me for everything. I leapt out, slammed the door furiously and started blaming her for everything. We shouted and yelled and carried on, and said a few things we've since lived to regret… well, you know what it's like when your grandma and I have one of our "events".

'Then there was a long and terrible silence, of a kind we had never known before. We refused to even look at each other. It was like all the stones in that desert went down our throats and into our hearts. We wanted to just sink into the ground and stay there forever.

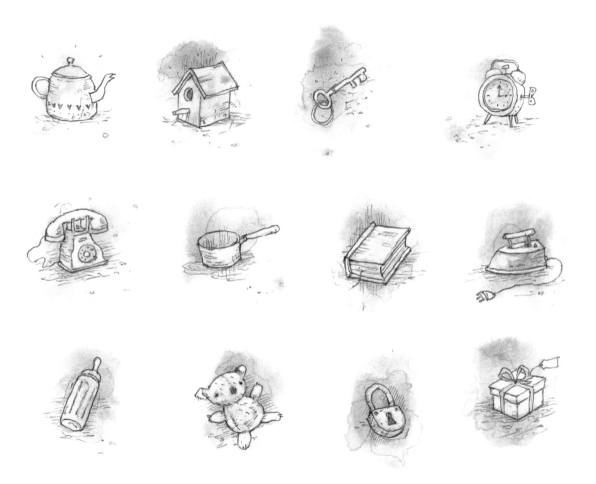

'Of course, as the light faded and the temperature dropped, we soon realised that we would have to do something quick-smart if we were to have any hope of returning to civilisation. And we'd have to do it together.

'The spare tyre – which we'd never needed before – was somehow rusted into the back of the car; it required the leverage of our combined weight on a crowbar to budge it. With one almighty heave it finally popped free. Our sense of relief was overwhelming. We almost didn't notice something twinkling in the hollow muddy pan of the car boot. Twinkling just like stars. Well, we rinsed off the mud with the last of the drinking water and still couldn't believe our eyes – two of the most perfect rings you ever saw! If you don't believe me, have a look at this!' Grandpa holds up his hand with a ring on it.

'From that moment on, we picked a random direction and took off at top speed, with a determination that could make any destination turn up on the far side of a bug-plastered windscreen. And sure enough, as we crested that last big hill, we could see all the lights of the outer suburbs unfold before us, streets like old friends, welcoming us home.

'By the time we pulled into the driveway, there was just enough time to shower, dress, exchange our vows and do all that ceremonial stuff we had rehearsed. It was as if we had been away for only a couple of hours, and everything was normal, with everyone saying "congratulations" over and over. Your grandma and I kept looking at each other, as though we had just returned from another planet.

'Anyway, that's pretty much it, the story of how we got married, beyond that big hill you can see from the window. Long before you lot came along.'

Grandpa shuffles off to the toilet, and then to check on his fruit trees. Admittedly, we are sceptical about everything we've heard, particularly as Grandpa can have a very lively imagination. There is only one thing to do – ask Grandma.

'Well, you know I rarely agree with your grandpa's account of *anything*,' she tells us. 'But in this case I'll make a rare exception.' And she shows us the other ring they found under the spare tyre, out in the desert.

no other country

the green painted concrete out the front of the house, which at first seemed like a novel way to save money on lawn-mowing, was now just plain depressing. The hot water came reluctantly to the kitchen sink as if from miles away, and even then without conviction, and sometimes a pale brownish colour. Many of the windows wouldn't open properly to let flies out. Others wouldn't shut properly to stop them getting in. The newly planted fruit trees died in the sandy soil of a too-bright backyard and were left like grave-markers under the slack laundry lines, a small cemetery of disappointment. It appeared to be impossible to find the right kinds of food, or learn the right way to say even simple things. The children said very little that wasn't a complaint.

'No other country is worse than this one,' their mother announced loudly and often, and nobody felt the need to challenge her.

After paying the mortgage, there was no money left to fix anything. 'You kids have to do more to help your mother,' their father kept saying, and this included going out to find the cheapest plastic Christmas tree available and storing it temporarily in the roof space. Here was something to look forward to at least, and the children spent the next month making their own decorations, cutting paper and foil into interesting shapes on the living room floor, and attaching pieces of thread. It helped them forget about the sweltering heat and all their troubles at school.

But when they went to get the tree down, they found it was stuck to the ceiling beams – it had been so hot up there that the plastic had actually *melted*. 'No other country is like this one!' muttered their mother. There was enough tree left to be worth salvaging, though, so the children set about scraping it free with butter knives. This was when the youngest stood on the weakest part of the ceiling, and his foot went straight through. What a disaster! Everyone was shouting and waving their hands: they all rushed down the ladder to inspect the damage from below; a hole that would undoubtedly cost a fortune to fix. But they couldn't find it. Confused, they rushed from room to room. Everywhere the ceiling was fine, no holes.

They went back up to check again where the foot had gone through – surely either in the laundry or kitchen? It was then that they were struck by a scent of grass, cool stone and tree sap that breezed through the attic. They all inspected the hole closely… It opened into another room altogether, one they didn't know about

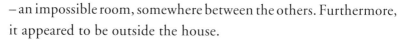

– an impossible room, somewhere between the others. Furthermore, it appeared to be outside the house.

This was how the family first discovered the place they later came to call 'the inner courtyard'. It was actually more like an old palace garden, with tall trees much older than any they had ever seen. There were ancient walls decorated with frescoes; the more they looked at them, the more the family recognised aspects of their own lives within these strange, faded allegories.

The seasons in their inner courtyard were reversed: here it was winter in summer; and later they would come to soak up the summer sun during the coldest, wettest part of the year. It was like being back in their home country, but also somewhere else, somewhere altogether different... And they would ponder this when unusual blossoms floated through the air on still evenings.
It became their special sanctuary. They visited at least twice a week for picnics, bringing everything they needed through the attic and

down a permanently installed ladder. They felt no need to question the logic of it, and simply accepted its presence gratefully.

It was decided to keep the inner courtyard a private family secret, although nobody said this explicitly – it just seemed the right thing to do. There was also a feeling that it was not *possible* to tell anyone else about it.

One day, however, the mother was stunned by a simple remark from an elderly Greek woman. They were talking over the back fence while hanging out laundry, and the neighbour said, 'We mostly have our barbecues in the inner courtyard, once we got the barbecue over, through the roof you know,' and laughed loudly.

At first the mother thought she had misheard, but when she described the inner courtyard of her own home, the Greek woman smiled and nodded. 'Yes, yes, every house here has the inner courtyard, if you can find it. Very strange, you know, because nowhere else has this thing. No other country.'

stick figures

if they are standing in the middle of the street, it's easy enough to drive around them, as you would a piece of cardboard or a dead cat. Turning your sprinklers on will discourage them from hanging around the front of your house; loud music and smoke from barbecues will also keep them away. They are not a problem, just another part of the suburban landscape, their brittle legs moving as slowly as clouds. They have always been here, since before anyone remembers, since before the bush was cleared and all the houses were built.

Adults pay them little attention. Young children sometimes dress them in old clothes and hats as if they were dolls or scarecrows, and are always scolded by parents, whose reasons are unclear. 'Just don't,' they say sternly.

Some older boys take great delight in beating them with baseball bats, golf clubs, or whatever is at hand, including the victim's own snapped-off limbs. With careful aim a good strike will send the head – a faceless clod of earth – flying high into the air. The body remains passively upright until smashed to splinters between heels and asphalt.

This can go on for hours, depending on how many the boys can find. But eventually it stops being amusing. It becomes boring, somehow enraging, the way they just stand there and take it. What are they? Why are they here? What do they want? Whack! Whack! Whack!

The only response is the sound of dead branches falling from old trees on windless evenings, and random holes appearing in front lawns, dark sockets where clods of earth have been removed during the night. And sure enough there they are again, standing by fences and driveways, in alleyways and parks, silent sentinels.

Are they here for a reason? It's impossible to know, but if you stop and stare at them for a long time, you can imagine that they too might be searching for answers, for some kind of meaning. It's as if they take all our questions and offer them straight back: Who are you? Why are you here? What do you want?

the
nameless
holiday

the nameless holiday happens once a year, usually around late August, sometimes October. It is always anticipated by children and adults alike with mixed emotion: it's not exactly festive, but still a celebration of sorts, the origin of which has been long forgotten.

All that is known are the familiar rituals: the laying out of one's most prized possessions on the bedroom floor; then choosing one special object – exactly the right one – and carrying it carefully up a ladder to the roof and leaving it under the TV aerial (already decorated with small shiny things such as chocolate wrappers, old CDs, and the tops off tubs of yoghurt, licked clean and threaded with string, tied with special slip-knots).

Then there is the traditional midnight picnic in the backyard, front lawn, or any place with a good view of one's own roof – across the street if necessary, which is why families sometimes gather by the roadside on blankets. Here are born fond memories of freshly baked gingerbread crows, hot pomegranate juice as tart as a knife and small plastic whistles, inaudible to the ears of both humans and dogs. Not to mention all that excited chatter and giggling, all that polite shushing, everyone struggling to observe the convention of silence.

Those who stay awake long enough are rewarded by a momentary sound that never fails to draw a sharp intake of breath – the delicate tapping of hoofs descending on roof tiles. It is always so startling, so hard to believe at first, like a waking dream or a rumour made solid. But sure enough, there he is, the reindeer with no name: enormous, blind as a bat, sniffing under the TV aerial with infinite animal patience. He always knows exactly which objects are so loved that their loss will be felt like the snapping of a cord to the heart, and it's only these that he nudges tenderly until they become hooked onto his great antlers. The rest he leaves alone, leaping gracefully back up into the cool darkness.

What a remarkable, unnameable feeling it is, right at the moment of his leaping: something like sadness and regret, of suddenly wanting your gift back and held tight to your chest, knowing that you will certainly never see it again. And then there is the letting go as your muscles release, your lungs exhale, and the backwash of longing leaves behind this one image on the shore of memory: a huge reindeer on your roof, bowing down.

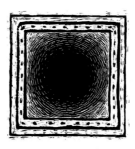

| | 8 | 6 | 4 | | 3 | 7 | 9 | 2 | 5 |
| 2 | 9 | 1 | 6 | 5 | 8 | 7 | 3 | 4 |

THOUGHT FOR THE DAY:
'A great deal of intelligence can be invested in ignorance when the need for illusion is deep.' - Saul Bellow

Div cover (Times)	Interest cover (Times)	Ret on Ord SHF %
n/c	17.10	45.17
18.96	7.32	11.00
1.43	1.28	20.44
2.25	1.30	19.76
1.11	3.57	21.41
0.90	1.24	19.21
1.73	1.24	22.61
n/c	27.31	43.15
2.94	5.63	24.03
1.93	5.07	23.45
2.00	31.75	34.41
4.32	12.66	23.74
2.45	1.40	24.69
.43	2.58	16.35
0.83	1.44	20.27
.73	1.21	21.08
.31	10.35	30.62
n/a	n/a	n/a
.60	5.38	9.22
.22	8.89	30.87
.46	3.93	12.92
.60	9.68	17.11
.30	6.92	29.88
.39	8.62	19.36
.91	13.26	29.01
.14	2.93	8.11
.22	6.81	13.25
.09	9.03	16.82
/c	0.44	-49.35
/c	7.15	19.39
.1	357.40	94.97
.7	5.05	25.18
.9	21.36	29.13
.3	2.35	6:57
.9	2.13	36.40
.1	3.84	14.00
.0	5.75	19.25
.c	3.34	45.14
	6.85	20.79
	4.38	12.51
	2.63	7.22
	3.57	14.54
	4.90	21.80
	0.73	-4.99
	15.98	34.40

The Amnesia Machine

It comes to me uninvited at the breakfast table, the recollection of a recurring dream so vivid that it feels almost like a real memory. It goes like this:

I AM STANDING in the middle of our street. In the distance I can see an enormous metal object, some kind of machine creeping down the road on the back of a long truck. It's the sweltering long weekend before the last election, and everyone has stopped washing cars, reading papers, watching sport or renovating bathrooms to come out and enjoy this unexplained spectacle. And to receive a free ice-cream, available from a colourful van that is never far away. It's playing a catchy jingle, one I know I've heard before.

A spectator in front of me says, 'Makes you truly appreciate the beauty of human engineering.'

The machine is close enough now to eclipse the sky, and I have to agree with him. It is massive, awe-inspiring, beyond the comprehension of ordinary tax-payers.

Further along, the truck backs into the treeless park behind our shopping centre. A team of construction workers are already waiting with an array of cranes and cables, and they set about shifting this monstrous thing onto an area of grass marked out with oily lines. There's a cacophony of hammering and welding. A big sign is bolted to a razor-wire fence: 'KEEP OUT'. Then there is silence. The workers are nowhere to be seen. I realise that it's already dark and everyone has gone home to eat dinner and watch the news.

Deep within the metal structure, lights are blinking to life and there's an electric humming noise, a thin vibration I can feel in my back teeth, and another swooshing sound, like cars on a freeway at night. Somewhere far away, a dog is barking.

I only recall this upon reading a newspaper article about the recent election result, an unsurprising government victory, and some other stories about media ownership, missing government revenue, corruption and so on, all quite boring. Almost every page features a full colour advertisement for a new, bright pink ice-cream.

Coming home from my weekly trip to the supermarket I decide to go the long way, by the park, out of curiosity. Of course there's nothing to see, just an empty square of freshly mown grass surrounded by a razor-wire fence, with a single sign that says 'KEEP OUT'. I think it's always been there, though I can't imagine why.

Now I'm here again in the kitchen, listening to the faint drone of a neighbour's TV (yet another current affairs show with a catchy jingle) and the soft rush of late evening traffic; an ocean of white noise.

I'm trying to recall my dream about that thing, that machine, but even now the details are elusive and my memory feels more and more like an emptying room.

All I can think about is the ice-cream cone right here in my hand, melting. Is it meant to be strawberry or raspberry?

Truth over-rated, explains M

THE MINISTER for Public Denials yesterday issued a press statement ahead of a government inquiry into government corruption, anticipating a finding that no such thing exists.

'I mean, what would you expect? Since our party purchased a new incinerator, there have been no records of any improper conduct

'Well let me just say this,' replied the Minister for the fifteenth time in as many minutes, 'While it may be clear, at this point in time, today, that certain statements were made which did not take into full account any actual correspondence to a layperson's definition of reality, it is the opinion of this government

so compared to telling the truth r dollar-for-dollar i

'And anywa with a bonus eve of ignorance. Fur ed to the incinera the kinky bird, recaptured only a month ago, has again escaped custody. Locals are warned not to approach the pink flamingo, which is considered by authorities to be 'highly dangerous' in the absence of any evidence to the contrary. 'It's only a matter of time before it kills a small child,' said one resident too afraid to be named.

tion with a glut of meaningless information.

'There should be no question of this corporation's commitment to clear communication,' he told reporters. 'We are multi-focused on the enhanced outcome of a high priority information distribution initiative driven by precisely articulated context sensitive delivery.'

unknown knowns m what we know to be and what we would rather not know.'

Elsewhere, in loc protesters have been silenced by the threa of court action and developers granted green-light for progr fast-tracked clearing in the interests of all shareholders.

'There is no prof in saving endangere They are going to all die sooner or later an Better to process the as burger patties.

In other news, to h weapons of mass dis distraction have been employed through the use of doublespeak, a embedded messages omission of facts with commercial television cross-media ownershi public ignorance is a legitimate weapon in war against terror.

'It is vitally impor that we continue to se find new enemies, and outside of our own co in order to maintain th greater political contro over our own citizens. repression of civil liber intellectual anaesthesia and reinforcement of o unquestioning faith in If you are not with us th damned as unpatriotic, of good and evil.'

Offshore torturing o zero accountability and steadfast denials. Subse to bomb neighbouring s yet to be voted on, as w backyard arms storage

Meltdown not so bad afte

er

failure, the same

xt week n claims e direct-

AS THE NATION faces its most devastating environmental crisis in history, the federal government has been quick to assert that unemployment is at an all-time low, due largely to a redefinition of the term 'employ-

Interest rates are also at their best since the last time they reached an equivalent level. 'And we are doing everything we can to fight terrorism,' assured a PR expert, 'a war that will almost certainly be over by Christmas

eclipsed by promises of sweeping tax cuts that w free beer in every fridge no child in poverty by th

alert but not alarmed

it's funny how these days, when every household has its own inter-continental ballistic missile, you hardly even think about them.

At first they were issued randomly. Back then it was exciting: someone you knew might get a letter from the government, and the truck dropped off their missile the following week. Then every corner house had to have one, then every second house, and now it would look strange if you didn't have a missile next to your garden shed or clothesline.

We understand well enough what they're for, at least in a broad sense. We know that we need to *protect our way of life in an increasingly dangerous climate*. We know that everyone must *participate in upholding our national security* (by taking the pressure off arms-storage facilities) and, most importantly, be rewarded with the feeling that we are *doing our bit*.

It's a modest commitment. We only have to wash and wax our missile on the first Sunday of every month and occasionally pull a dipstick out the side to check the oil level. Every couple of years a tin of paint appears in a cardboard box on the doorstep, which means it's time to remove any rust and give the missile a fresh coat of gunmetal grey.

A lot of us, though, have started painting the missiles different colours, even decorating them with our own designs, like butterflies or stencilled flowers. They take up so much space in the backyard, they might as well look nice, and the government leaflets don't say that you *have* to use the paint they supply.

We're now also in the habit of stringing lights on them at Christmas time. You should go up the hill at night to see the hundreds of sparkling spires all around, twinkling and flashing.

Plus there are plenty of very good *practical* uses for a backyard missile. If you unscrew the lower panel and take the wires and stuff out, you can use the space to grow seedlings or store garden tools, clothes pegs and firewood. With a more extensive renovation, it also makes an excellent 'space rocket' cubby house, and if you own a dog, you'll never need to buy a kennel. One family has even turned theirs into a pizza oven, hollowing out the top part for a chimney.

Yes, we all know that there's a good chance the missiles won't work properly when the government people finally come to get them, but over the years we've stopped worrying about that. Deep down, most of us feel it's probably better this way. After all, if there are families in far away countries with their own backyard missiles, armed and pointed back at us, we would hope that they too have found a much better use for them.

wake

on a cold night last winter there was a fire at the house of a man who only days before had beaten his dog to death.

Being a strong man, he was able to rescue all his belongings single-handedly, carrying them out of the burning building and onto the front lawn. As soon as he had finished, a hundred dogs of every shape and size trotted into the flickering light from the surrounding shadows and promptly sat on top of every appliance and piece of furniture as if it were their own. They would not let the man come close and snapped at him viciously when he tried to hit them, but otherwise remained still, staring impassively at the flames.

The fire burned with astonishing intensity, the house collapsed within minutes, and the enraged man stormed away in search of a weapon. As if on cue, the dogs leapt to the ground and circled quietly in the smoky darkness, taking turns to urinate on every rescued object. They howled once, not very loud or long, but with such melancholy that even those who could not hear it turned restlessly in their sleep.

And then they were gone, scattering to the streets and alleys, heads hanging at the sound of their own paws scuffing on the concrete footpaths, ground that had once been wild black earth. They did not look back at the final small fires on the lawn, or the man who returned with a useless crowbar to stand in the ash, alone and weeping. The dogs thought only of home: the smell of warm kennels, of safe laundry blankets and the beds of sleeping humans, the ones who had given them peculiar names.

Seal your box up with packing tape,* punch an air-hole in the top and pop a straw in.

*if you don't have any, try chewing gum.

super!

5. Pick a quiet spot in your backyard, grab a spade and dig a neat box-sized hole.

Draw a picture of your pet on the side. Crayons are good for this.

6. Find any old birthday cards and saved candle stubs and put them in the bottom. Used gift wrapping also makes excellent fertiliser. Now carefully plant your box, making sure the straw is exposed.

nobody is around

first that

checking

Water gently with warm herbal tea.

8. Whisper a secret (or two)

9.

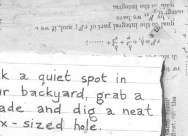

Go to bed and imagine all the games you can play with your pet, until you fall asleep.

10.

THE NEXT MORNING

THE NEXT NEXT MORNING THE NEXT

THE NEXT MORNING

MORNING

NEXT MORNING

THE NEXT MORNING

AND THEN...

WITH ENOUGH CARE

EVEN THE MOST UNLOVED OBJECTS CAN BECOME YOUR PERFECT ANIMAL COMPANION.

THE NEXT MORNI MORNING THE NEXT M MORNING

mintox!

our expedition

my brother and I could easily spend hours arguing about the correct lyrics to a TV jingle, the impossibility of firing a gun in outer space, where cashew nuts come from, or whether we really did see a saltwater croc in the neighbour's pool that one time. Once we had a huge argument about why the street directory in Dad's car stopped at Map 268. It was my contention that *obviously* certain pages had fallen out. Map 268 itself was packed full of streets, avenues, crescents and cul-de-sacs, right up to the edge – I mean, it's not like it faded off into nothing. It made no sense.

Yet my brother insisted, with an irritating tone of authority enjoyed by many older siblings, that the map was literally correct, because it would otherwise have 'joins Map 269' in small print up the side. If the map says it is so, then so it is. My brother was like this about most things. Annoying.

Verbal combat ensued;
'It's right' – 'it's not' – ' it is'
– 'not' – 'is' – 'not' – a ping-
pong mantra performed while
eating dinner, playing computer
games, brushing teeth or lying
wide awake in bed, calling
out through the thin partition
between our rooms until Dad
got angry and told us to stop.

Eventually we decided there
was only one solution: go and see
for ourselves. We shook hands
over a mighty twenty-dollar bet,
a staggering amount to gamble
even on a sure thing, and planned
an official scientific expedition
to the mysterious outer suburbs.

My brother and I took the
number 441 bus as far as it
would go and set off on foot
after that. We had filled our
backpacks with all the necessities
for such a journey: chocolate,
orange juice, little boxes of
sultanas and, of course, the
contentious street directory.

It was exciting to be on a real expedition, like venturing into a desert or jungle wilderness, only much better sign-posted. How great it must have been long ago, before shops and freeways and fast-food outlets, when the world was still unknown. Armed with sticks we hacked our way through slightly overgrown alleys, followed our compass along endless footpaths, scaled multi-level car parks for a better view and made careful notes in an exercise book. Despite starting out bright and early, however, we were nowhere near the area in question by mid-afternoon, when we had planned to be already back home on our beanbags, watching cartoons.

The novelty of our adventure was wearing thin, but not because our feet hurt and we were constantly blaming each other for the forgotten sunscreen. There was some other thing that we could not clearly explain. The further we ventured, the more everything looked the same, as if each new street, park or shopping mall was simply another version of our own, made from the same giant assembly kit. Only the names were different.

By the time we reached the last uphill stretch, the sky was turning pink, the trees dark, and we were both looking forward to nothing more than sitting down and resting our feet. The inevitable victory speech I had been mentally preparing all along now seemed like a meaningless bunch of words. I wasn't in the mood for gloating.

I guess my brother felt much the same. Always the impatient walking companion, he was some distance ahead, and by the time I caught up he was sitting with his back to me, right in the middle of the road, *with his legs hanging over the edge.*

'I guess I owe you twenty bucks,' I said.

'Yup,' he said.

One annoying thing I forgot to mention about my brother: he is almost always right.

night of the
turtle rescue

the night of the turtle rescue, I thought we were going to die. I was clutching my hair and repeating the same questions over and over again: Why do I always listen to your insane plans? Why aren't we at home watching TV like everyone else? What possible difference will any of this make? I looked back and saw our pursuers relentlessly closing in, so much bigger and more powerful than we young fools with our pathetic ideals. 'It's all over!' I yelled at the top of my voice. 'Let's give ourselves up while we still have a chance!' And then, illuminated by the sweep of fierce searchlights, I saw our cargo for the first time: tiny limbs struggling to hold on, small unreadable faces staring out in all directions, voiceless mouths opening and closing. Nine small turtles – all we managed to save – just those nine. They turned their heads, looking back at me with eyes like black buttons, like full stops, blinking. I could think of only one thing, and it erupted from my lungs like a fireball as we hurtled into the darkness: 'Keep going! Keep going! Keep going!'

Warm Regards from our Tuesday Afternoon Reading Group !

PUBLIC LIBRARY SERVICE
OF OUTER SUBURBIA

This book is due for return on or before the last date stamped below.

In the meantime, the author wishes to thank the following people and organisations for their generous assistance and support:

Inari Kiuru. Sophie Byrne. Jodie Webster. Rosalind Price. Helen Chamberlin. Mum & Dad. Arthur A Levine. Jasmine Yee. Makiko Hattori. Craig Silvey. Sheralyn Bavinton. Sarah Brenan. Jennifer Castles. Peter Stoakes. Susannah Chambers. Erica Wagner. Sue Flockhart. Andrea McNamara. Jenni Walker. Michael Killalea. Susan, Greg, Dan, Rachel & Lucas Marie. Clare Webster. Mary Anne Butler. Trent Dhue. Terry Morgan. Fiona Carter. Dyan Blacklock. The Fremantle Children's Literature Centre. Books Illustrated, The A.S.A. and the State Libraries of Western Australia and Victoria. Sarah Tran.

LB14L   CP2216 16

in memory of Eddie budgie champion

This project has been assisted by the Australian Government through the Australia Council, its arts funding and advisory body.

Australian Government

Australia Council for the Arts

Significant Author